Mango, Mango

Written by Anne Schreiber
Pictures by Keiko Narahashi

SCHOLASTIC INC.
New York   Toronto   London   Auckland   Sydney

Copyright © 1994 by Scholastic Inc.
All rights reserved. Published by Scholastic Inc.
Printed in the U.S.A.
ISBN 0-590-27367-1
ISBN 0-590-29227-7 (meets NASTA specifications)

2 3 4 5 6 7 8 9 10   09   01 00 99 98 97 96 95 94

Mango, mango
Red and shining
Gold and shining
Mango, mango.

That sweet syrup
Sticky, sticky
Sticky, sticky
Sweet, sweet syrup.

4

Down my chin
Drippy, drippy
Drippy, drippy
Thick and thin.

In the forest
Trees are blooming
Birds are flying
Mango forest.

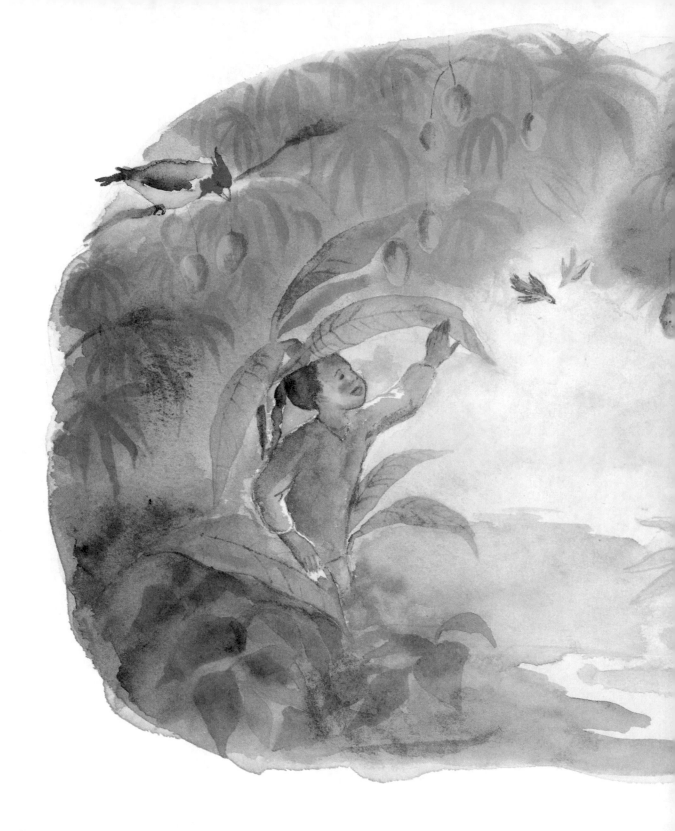

Monkeys swinging
Buzz bees stinging
Birds are singing
On the wind.

Wind is blowing
Fruit is falling
Mango's calling
Calls to me.

Mango, mango
Sweet and sticky
Sticky, drippy
Sweet fruit tree.